michael morpurgo

Mudpuddle Farm

Alien Invasion!

Illustrated by Shoo Rayner

HarperCollins *Children's Books*

Martians at Mudpuddle Farm first published in hardback by
A&C Black (Publishers) Limited 1994
First published in paperback by Collins, a division of
HarperCollins, 1995

Mum's the Word first published in hardback by
A&C Black (Publishers) Limited 1995
First published in paperback by Collins, a division of
HarperCollins, 1996

This bind-up edition first published in Great Britain by
HarperCollins *Children's Books* in 2008
First published in the United States of America in this edition by
HarperCollins *Children's Books* 2018
HarperCollins *Children's Books* is a division of HarperCollins*Publishers* Ltd,
HarperCollins Publishers
1 London Bridge Street
London SE1 9GF

The HarperCollins website address is:
www.harpercollins.co.uk
1

ISBN 978–0–00–826910–4

Printed and bound in Great Britain by CPI Group (UK) Ltd, Croydon CR0 4YY

Find out more about HarperCollins and the environment at
www.harpercollins.co.uk/green

For all the children who come to
Farms for City Children at Treginnis—M. M.

For Isabelle Honey—S. R.

Contents

Martians at Mudpuddle Farm

Chapter One

There was once a family of all kinds
of animals that lived in the farmyard
behind the tumbledown barn on
Mudpuddle Farm.

WAKE UP, YOU SLEEPY HEADS.

At first light every morning Frederick,
the flame-feathered rooster, lifted his
eyes to the sun and crowed and crowed
until the light came on in old Farmer
Rafferty's bedroom window.

One by one the animals crept out into the dawn and stretched

and yawned

and scratched themselves.

But no one ever spoke a word—not until
after breakfast.

Early one morning, old Farmer Rafferty
looked out of his window. The corn was
waving yellow in the sun. The stream
ran clear and silver under the bridge,
and the air was humming with summer.

The bees will be out flying today,
and that means honey. And honey means
money, and I need to buy a
new tractor. The old one won't start in
the mornings like it should. Get busy,
bees. Buzz my beauties, buzz!

Chapter Two

Deep in the beehive at the bottom of the apple orchard, Little Bee was getting ready for his first solo flight.

Now remember, load up your pollen in the clover field, and then come straight home. And don't get lost. Good luck.

Good luck!

And off flew Little Bee out into the wide blue sky. Around and around he flew, looking for the clover field, but he couldn't find it anywhere.

Buzz

Buzz

Buzz

Buzz

Buzz

Buzz

There's a cat down there. I'll ask him.

So he buzzed down toward the old tractor where Mossop, the cat with the one and single eye, was trying hard not to wake up.

Mossop opened his eye.

Then he went back to sleep again.

The trouble was that Little Bee didn't know his right from his left or his left from his right.

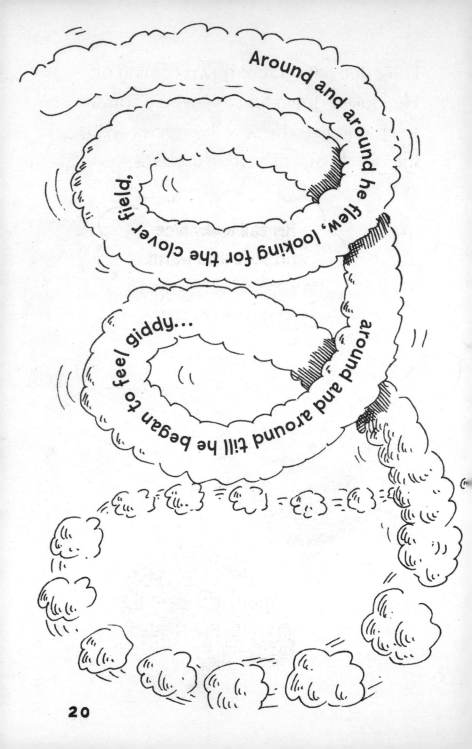

Around and around he flew, looking for the clover field, around and around till he began to feel giddy...

20

Little Bee felt a great yawn coming on.
He looked down for somewhere soft to
sleep and then he saw the tractor with
the old cat still asleep on the seat.

His tail looks nice
and soft and warm.
He won't mind—he won't
even know I'm there.

And he was quite right about that.
Mossop never even felt Little Bee
land on his tail. He was too busy
dreaming. So Little Bee and Mossop
snoozed together in the sun and the
hours passed.

Chapter Three

Back in the beehive, Queen Bee was getting worried. Little Bee had been gone for hours now and something had to be done. She called all her bees together.

Right, forget pollen-gathering, forget honey-making. Little Bee is lost and we've got to find him before dark else he'll get cold and die. Follow me.

Ah-ha! Once more unto the breach!

Old Farmer Rafferty was milking Auntie Grace, the dreamy-eyed cow, when he heard the bees coming. "There they go," he chortled over his milk pail.

And then he began to sing as he often did when he was happy. He sang in a crusty, croaky kind of a voice, and he made it up as he went along.

Honey honey bee, be my honey bee, be my honey bunch, be my Queen Bee...

Great words!

Shame about the tune!

Out in the clover field, Diana the
silly sheep

was rolling on her back

to scratch her itches

when she saw a great swarm of bees
coming straight toward her.

She struggled to her feet and ran off
toward the pond as fast as her legs
could carry her. No one was at all
surprised when she jumped right in.
That's what she always did when
there were bees around.

As usual it was Jigger, the almost-always-sensible sheepdog, who had to pull her out.

Silly sheep!

They can't sting you in the water. That's what my mother told me.

"And some mothers do have them," thought Albertine from her island in the pond.

It's just bees buzzing. Nothing to worry about.

That's my mom!

She's so calm in a crisis!

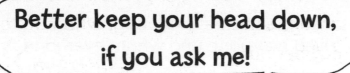

said
Upside
and Down.

So the two white ducks that no one could tell apart upside-downed themselves in the pond and stayed there all day long.

And, sure enough, the sky above them suddenly darkened and the humming became a droning and the droning became a roaring.

DON'T MOVE!

But no one could move anyway. They were all too terrified, except Albertine, of course.

"Albertine," said Captain without moving his lips. "What are we going to do?"

Chapter Four

Albertine thought her deep goosey thoughts for a moment. Then she said, "Just follow me." And she swam across the pond, waddled through the open gate and out into the cornfield beyond.

All the animals followed because they knew that Albertine was the most intelligent goose that ever lived. If anyone knew what to do, she would. They reached the middle of the cornfield and looked up. The bees were still following them.

Albertine began to run
around in a great big circle.

All the animals did the same, running
around and around.

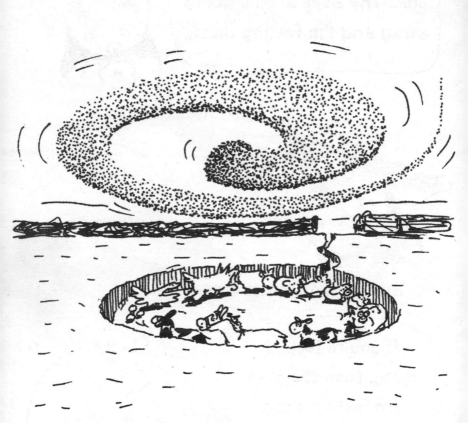

And above them the bees all flew
around and around and around.

I wish someone would tell me why we're doing this. The bees aren't going away and I'm feeling dizzy.

said Auntie Grace.

Me too, dear!

said Primrose.

"Good," said Albertine.

If you're feeling dizzy, then the bees are feeling dizzy.

She's so logical!

Not many people know this, but when a bee feels dizzy, he gets sleepy too; and then he'll buzz off home to sleep. Never fails—you'll see. Keep going.

So around and around they all ran until suddenly the buzzing stopped. When they looked up, the bees had all buzzed off, just as Albertine had said they would.

How do you do it?

It's called genius!

She's a wonderful mother too!

And so modest.

Chapter Five

The bees were flying home over the farmyard when one of them suddenly spotted Little Bee all curled up asleep on Mossop's tail.

ma'am!

"Follow me," said Queen Bee and down they flew.

LITTLE BEE

"I got lost," cried Little Bee.

I want to go home.

"Soon," Queen Bee yawned. She could hardly keep her eyes open, she was so sleepy.

But first we'll hang around here and have a little snooze.

And so that's what they all did. Soon there was a great ball of snoozing bees hanging on Mossop's tail.

MEANWHILE...

Back in the cornfield, Captain had a worried look on his face. "Just look what we've done to Farmer Rafferty's corn," he said. "Just look." And they looked.

They had flattened out a huge circle in the corn. Not a single solitary stalk still stood standing.

They all heard him. He was walking into
the field singing his honey song.

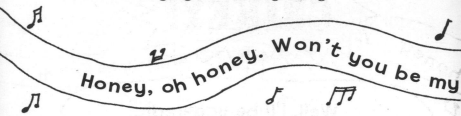

Honey, oh honey. Won't you be my

When Farmer Rafferty reached the
middle of the cornfield, there wasn't an
animal to be found. What he did find
was a great circle of flattened corn.

And he began to chortle and his eyes
began to twinkle.

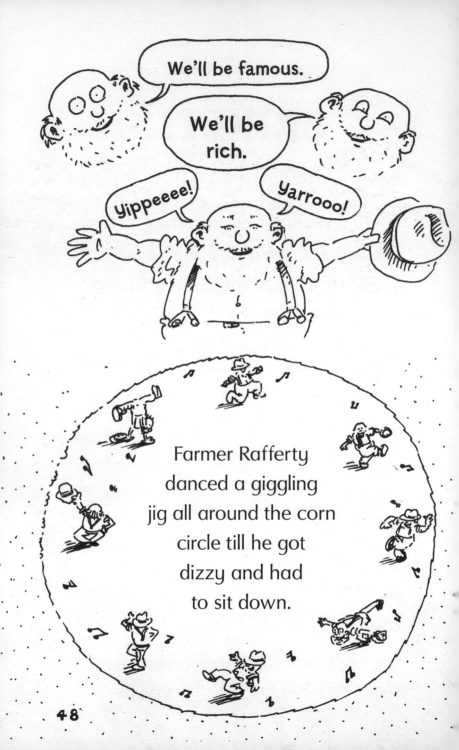

Farmer Rafferty
danced a giggling
jig all around the corn
circle till he got
dizzy and had
to sit down.

Then off he went toward the farmhouse, counting on his fingers and muttering to himself.

He didn't know it, but from behind the farmyard wall, the animals were watching and listening to every word.

"What's a Martian?" Diana asked, and of course everyone looked at Albertine.

"Well," she said, thinking very hard indeed, "they walk stiffly like robots do and they carry ray guns like Farmer Rafferty says." The animals could hardly believe it, but if Albertine had told them, then it had to be true. After all, there was nothing Albertine didn't know.

Chapter Six

Farmer Rafferty was still counting on his fingers when he passed by the old tractor and noticed the ball of bees hanging on Mossop's tail.

Oh, dear me. My bees have gone and swarmed. Perhaps they couldn't find the way back home. I'll have to put them back in their hive.

And he disappeared inside the farmhouse.

While he was gone, the animals crept
back into the farmyard, just in time to
notice something coming in through the
farmyard gate. It was dressed in white
from head to toe.

It wore a white helmet ★

and white gloves ★

and it walked stiffly like a robot, ★

and as it walked it puffed smoke ★
out of its ray gun.

In its other hand it carried ★
a great big sack.

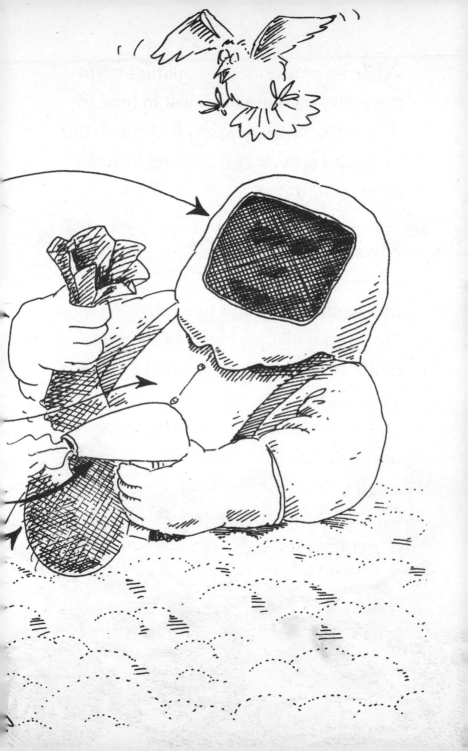

A Martian!

Diana cried. And she ran—they all ran.
They ran until they came to the edge
of the pond where they found Albertine
washing herself.

"It's a Martian," panted Jigger the almost-always-sensible sheepdog.

Albertine smiled her goosey smile.

Look again.

That's not a Martian,
that's old Farmer
Rafferty in his
bee-keeping costume.
Now watch...

And they watched as old Farmer
Rafferty puffed smoke around the
swarm of bees.

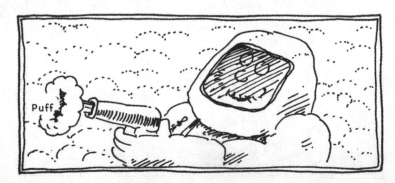

Farmer Rafferty scooped the bees into his sack, and off he went singing his honey song, with Queen Bee and Little Bee and all the others still snoozing inside.

Chapter Seven

Later that afternoon the first cars
arrived. Before long, Front Meadow
was filled edge to edge with cars,
and there were people everywhere.
Mossop, who had woken up by now,
walked down the lane and met Jigger
and the others.

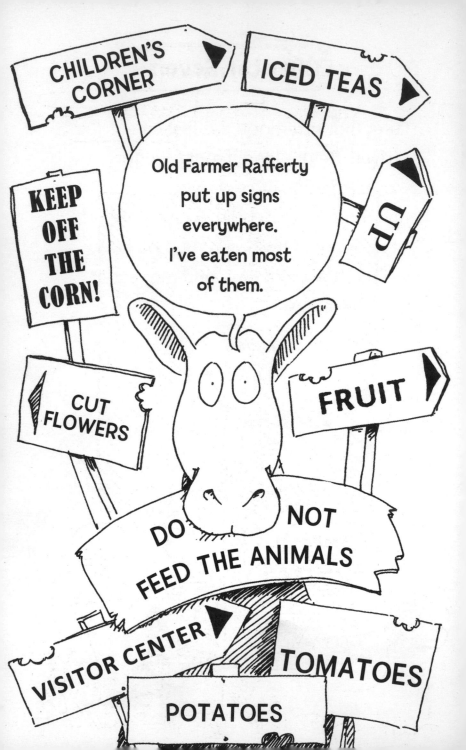

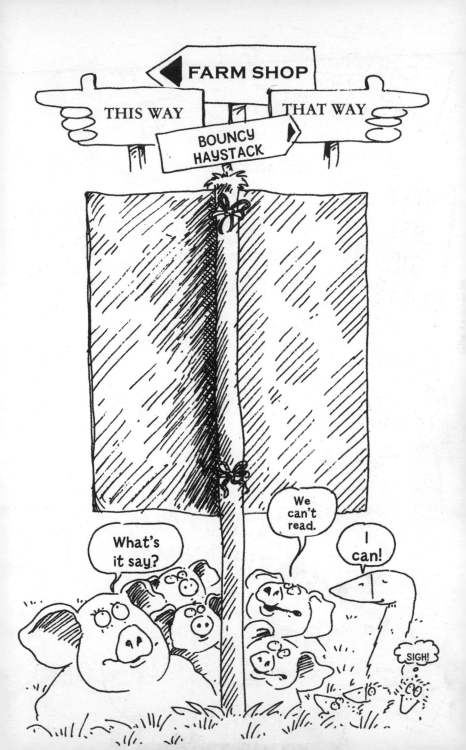

It says...

RAFFERTY'S CORN CIRCLE

GENUINE
MARTIAN CORN CIRCLE

To Visit .... Two Dollars

Parking .... Two Dollars

Martian Milkshake ..... Two Dollars

Honey Cookies .... Two Dollars

"No one's going to believe a silly story like that, are they?" said Jigger; but when Albertine looked at him he wished he hadn't said it.

"I think," said Albertine, "that we believe mostly what we want to believe."

Chapter Eight

That afternoon Farmer Rafferty showed all the visitors around his Martian corn circle.

After that they settled down on the
front lawn to Martian treats.

He told them the story of the flying
saucer and the Martians that had
landed on Mudpuddle Farm, and they
swallowed it all (the treats and the
story) and went home happy.

And old Farmer Rafferty was happy too. He'd soon have enough money to buy his new tractor.

It would be all red and shiny, with a cab on it so he could plow his fields without getting wet and so Mossop could sleep out of the wind.

But Mossop was quite happy out on the old tractor in the farmyard. None of the animals ever told him about the day the bees swarmed on his tail. They thought it might give him bad dreams, and they didn't want that.

The night came down, the moon came up and everyone slept on Mudpuddle Farm.

Mum's the word

Chapter One

There was once a family of all kinds of animals that lived in the farmyard behind the tumbledown barn on Mudpuddle Farm.

You are the sunshine of my life...

At first light every morning Frederick, the flame-feathered rooster, lifted his eyes to the sun and crowed and crowed until the light came on in old Farmer Rafferty's bedroom window.

One...by...one, the animals crept out
into the dawn...

...and stretched...

...and yawned...

...and scratched themselves.

But no one ever spoke a word, not until
after breakfast.

One morning, Captain was crunching away at his last mouthful of breakfast hay when he noticed something was wrong.

Someone was missing. **Gone!**

Albertine and her little goslings were preening themselves on their island.

Upside and Down were upside down in the pond.

Peggoty and her little piglets, including Pintsize, snuffled and snorted around the dunghill.

Diana the silly sheep, who couldn't count to save her life, was counting the clouds.

I wish I was like a fluffy little cloud.

You are!

Penelope and her chicks scratched and scuffled in the orchard, never too far from Frederick.

Auntie Grace and Primrose grazed nose to nose in the meadow.

Jigger, the almost-always-sensible sheepdog, was chasing his tail again.

And Mossop, the cat with the one and single eye, was curled up asleep on his tractor seat as he always was.

BUT, where was Egbert the grumbly goat?

Jigger, have you seen that grumbly goat?

Nope, I'll have a look, okay?

So Jigger looked and looked.

Egbert wasn't anywhere. He'd skipped out, buzzed off, gone walkabout.

If anyone knows where he is, thought Jigger, *Albertine will, because Albertine always knows everything.* So Jigger ran down to the pond.

But Egbert did not come back. The animals searched here, there and everywhere for him.

But it was no good, he couldn't find him anywhere. No one could find him.

"I can't think of where he's gone," said Auntie Grace the dreamy-eyed brown cow. "Nor me," said Primrose, who always agreed with her.

I don't know where he's gone either.

"I know, I know," said Diana the silly sheep.

He's gone missing!

"Don't worry," Albertine told her little goslings.

That goat will be back, you'll see, around suppertime, I should think.

She's so reassuring.

Chapter Two

Sure enough, just as old Farmer Rafferty
was giving all the animals their supper
that evening, Egbert wandered into the
yard, grumbling as usual.

I'm tummy-rumbling hungry.
I've hardly eaten all day.
Where's my din-din?

Groan

Gurgle

Rumble

Rumble

Gurgle

Groan

"Egbert, where have you been?" asked Farmer Rafferty in the nasty, raspy voice he kept for special occasions.

I've been looking for you everywhere!

"We were worried sick," said Captain, the carthorse that everyone loved and who loved everyone.

But Egbert wouldn't say another word
about it.

Down on her island in the pond,
Albertine shook her head, smiled
her goosey smile and thought deep
goosey thoughts.

I told you he'd come back, didn't I?
I'll tell you something else too, just so
long as you keep mum, if you know
what I mean. That goat's been
up to something.

What? What? What?

Who knows? Who knows?
Now, let's watch the sun go down,
and then we'll all go to sleep.

Chapter Three

It wasn't long after this that Egbert
began behaving very strangely indeed.
For one thing, he stopped grumbling.
Everyone thought he must be sick, but
he wasn't.

Are you
feeling all right,
Egbert?

Enigmatic smile

"Good morning," he'd say as he passed by,

... and isn't it a fine one too?

Isn't it a good day to be alive?

And he'd say that with the wind whistling through the farmyard and the rain thundering down on the corrugated roofs.

Then one day Diana the silly sheep
saw something very, very strange.
She saw Egbert dancing! And he was
singing too!

Of course, none of the animals believed
her at first, because Diana was always
silly. But she told them and told them
until they had to come and look.

And of course, when they saw it with their own eyes they had to believe it. Egbert was dancing in the puddles, and singing his heart out.

"He's really sick,"
said Jigger sadly.

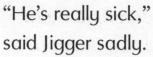

"Hope it's not catching," said Penelope,
hurrying her chicks away.

"He's gone loopy, if you ask me," said
Peggoty, keeping her distance at the top
of the dunghill.

Mossop opened his one and single eye
and shut it again.

I'm having a bad dream
about a singing, dancing
goat that's lost his
marbles. I think he ought
to see a vet.

But Auntie Grace and Primrose liked
the song so much that they found a
puddle of their own and joined in.

Albertine sighed and smiled
secretly to herself.

"You'd never understand, Captain," said
Albertine; and Captain felt very stupid.

Captain couldn't understand what
Albertine was talking about, but he
didn't want to say so in case she might
think he was as stupid as he felt he was.

Chapter Four

It was Tuesday, and Tuesday was always the day old Farmer Rafferty went off to market.

He put on his best jacket and his best hat. Then he scooped Mossop off his tractor seat and drove to market.

Off he went, happy as a lark, singing to himself as he always did when he was happy, though he could never remember the words.

I'm singing in the rain... I'm hum ti tum...

But old Farmer Rafferty had forgotten something else too. Something much more important than the words. He had forgotten to close his vegetable garden gate.

Later that morning, Egbert was feeling even hungrier than usual.

I've chewed the last of the paint off the gate. I've eaten the last of the paper bags. I've nearly eaten my rope, but I'm still hungry.

CREAK

RUMBLE

GROAN

Then he saw Farmer Rafferty's garden gate swinging in the wind, squeaking on its hinges.

Carrots, he thought. *Apples.*

No one saw him
tippy-toeing out
of the farmyard
except Mossop, who
happened to open his one and single
eye as Egbert passed by.

My goat dream
again, only now he's
on his tippy-toes and
ballet-dancing!

And he went back to sleep to finish his
dream.

All morning long, Egbert chomped and chewed his way through old Farmer Rafferty's carrots. No one noticed what he was up to until after lunch.

Early in the afternoon, Peggoty was taking her piglets for a stroll. As usual Pintsize had run on ahead. That was why he reached the garden gate first. Pintsize knew, and all the animals knew, that none of them (except Mossop because he was special), was ever allowed inside old Farmer Rafferty's vegetable garden.

Afternoon, Mossop.

So when he saw Egbert standing in the middle of the vegetable garden with a carrot in his mouth, he knew that there was going to be trouble, big trouble.

Pintsize loved it when other animals got into trouble for a change.

Peggoty could not believe her eyes. There wasn't a single carrot left except the one in Egbert's mouth.

Is something the matter, Peggoty?

The little piglets gasped. Peggoty let out her screechiest scream and called for help.

And all the animals came running as
fast as they could.

"Egbert!" cried Captain. "Out of there! Out of there! If old Farmer Rafferty catches you in his vegetable garden your goose will be cooked!" And then he thought about what he'd said.

> Oh, I'm sorry, Albertine.

But Albertine just smiled.

> See? I told you, Captain, didn't I? Carrots.

But Captain still didn't understand.

"I'll get him out," said Jigger the almost-always-sensible sheepdog. He dashed into the garden and tried to pull Egbert out by his rope. But Egbert would not budge.

Captain came in to help as well, but still Egbert dug his heels in and would not move.

Oh, come on, Egbert. Old Farmer Rafferty will be back in a minute.

In fact, old Farmer Rafferty was just at the end of the farm lane, talking to Farmer Farley from the next-door farm. "Goats," Farmer Farley was saying, "who'd have them? They go where they want, eat what they want, do as they please. Still they make you laugh, don't they?" And the two of them just laughed and laughed.

Back in the farmyard, the animals all heard Farmer Rafferty coming up the lane on his tractor. He was still singing away.

"I'm off," said Jigger.

"Me too," said Captain.

But Albertine decided to wait. "I think I'll just stay and see what happens," she said.

Pintsize hid under Albertine's wings and pretended to be a gosling.

As old Farmer Rafferty came through the garden gate, all the animals hid behind the wall and watched.

Suddenly, old Farmer Rafferty stopped singing. With bated breath, the animals waited for him to shout in his nasty, raspy voice. But he didn't.

All he said was:

You silly old goat, eating all my lovely carrots. Still, I expect you need them more than I do.

And Farmer Rafferty laughed and laughed. He picked up Egbert's rope and led him out into the orchard.

You have all the apples you can find, my dear. You'll get fat, but that doesn't matter, does it? You eat as much as you like.

The animals could not believe their ears. They could not understand it at all. But Albertine could. She smiled her goosey smile and waddled off back to her pond. Then she climbed up on to her island and tucked her head under her wing and slept. There were four little goslings under her wing that night, and one of them had hooves.

Chapter Five

It turned out just as old Farmer Rafferty had said. Egbert did get fat, very fat. It wasn't surprising—he did nothing but eat all day long.

He ate anything and everything—

Captain's
best hay,

Jigger's
biscuits,

Peggoty's
pigmeal,

Penelope's
corn,

Diana's
sheepnuts...

and old Farmer Rafferty's socks off the washing line.

He even ate the sack that Mossop used for his bed on the tractor seat.

"I'm not dreaming this," said Mossop, yawning hugely. "That goat is eating my bed." Mossop was not at all happy about that.

Right, that's the last straw. What are we going to do about that goat?

No one knew what to do, but they
all knew something had to be done.
So they went off to ask Albertine. If
anyone knew what to do, she would.

But Albertine was being very
secretive. "Mum's the word," she said
inscrutably, and she would say no
more.

"Well, I think that goat needs to lose some weight," said Auntie Grace the dreamy-eyed brown cow.

And I agree. He's almost as fat as we are, and we are cows. We're supposed to be fat.

But how do you get thin if you're fat?

"Jogging," said Jigger.

I do it all the time. That'll soon
cut him down to size. We'll jog him
around the front meadow five times
a day—that'll do the trick. And we'll
all do aerobics with him.
He'd like that.

So five times a day all the animals,
except Albertine, who thought it was all
very silly, jogged around Front Meadow.
Afterwards they did their aerobics, and
all the while Egbert would sing along
quite happily, and dance in
any puddles he could find.

Ridiculous!

"I'm singing in the sun, singing in the sun..." (or rain, depending on the weather). He didn't seem to mind the exercise at all, just so long as he could keep on eating afterwards.

And that's just what he did. He got fatter,

and fatter,

and fatter.

And, to everyone's amazement, he stopped grumbling completely. The animals could not believe it.

"I'm just the happiest, luckiest goat
in the whole wide world," he said,
jumping into another puddle.

"What's he got to be so happy about?"
said Jigger. "What's happened to him?"
And he went to ask Albertine again.

But Albertine was keeping mum. "Mum's the word," she said inscrutably, and she smiled a secret goosey smile again.

?

Mum's the word.

Twirl

Inscrutable means "seriously unfeatherable".

You're so smart, Pintsize.

He'll never make it to gosling school!

Chapter Six

Then one morning, Captain was looking out of his stable after his breakfast, when he saw that Egbert had vanished again.

Not again!

Gone!

No one could find him anywhere. All day long they looked but they still couldn't find him.

Egbert, where are you?

It's breakfast, Eggers!

Yoohoo, Egbert!

At last they went to tell old Farmer
Rafferty the bad news.

We've lost him again! We've lost Egbert!

But instead of saddling Captain and
going out to look for him, old Farmer
Rafferty just leant on his spade and
laughed and laughed.

Why don't
you have a
look through
my sitting-room
window?

Pow

Zip

Jigger got there first.

I don't believe it! He's got to be kidding!

What is it?

Kids! Egbert has had two kids!

But he can't! It's impossible!

"Oh, yes, he can," laughed old Farmer Rafferty. "He can and he has because *he* is a *she*. Egbert is Egberta, and she's just had two lovely kids."

And they all peered in at the window. There was Egberta lying out on the sofa, a cushion under her head, with her two little kids beside her.

That evening, Farmer Farley brought
Billy, his billy goat, over to Farmer
Rafferty's to see his kids.

"It's my Egberta who's the smart one,
bless her," said Farmer Rafferty.

"I'd say they're both smart," said
Farmer Farley.

Meanwhile, Billy chewed the paint off
the window and Egberta chewed the
sofa, and both of them looked very
happy indeed.

Chapter Seven

Out on the pond, Upside and Down came up for a breather. "Anything new happened?" they asked.

Egbert's not fat any more.

You're kidding!

"Not me," Albertine smiled. "Egberta. She's the one that's kidding. It'll be nice to have some real kids around, won't it, children?"

She cuddled her goslings under her wings, including the one with the hooves. "Do you want a story to send you to sleep?" And of course they did.

The night came down, the moon came up and everyone slept on Mudpuddle Farm.

Have you got them all?

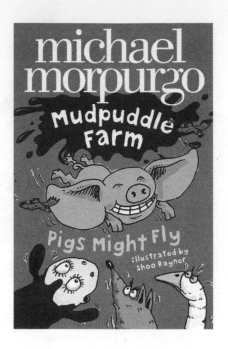

And Pigs Might Fly!

It's a long hot summer, and Pintsize the piglet
wonders if it might be cooler in the sky.
But when he tries to fly he annoys just
about everyone. It's time he learned his lesson...

Jigger's Day Off

Jigger the sheepdog has just one day off a year.
Just one day to chase all those little animals
hiding in the corn. But even the best
plans go wrong...

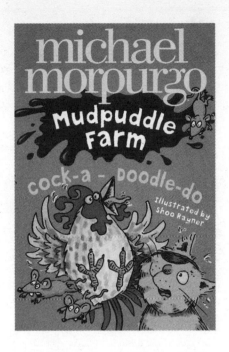

Mossop's Last Chance

Mossop the old farm cat likes to sleep—and not much else! So when Farmer Rafferty tells him to catch twenty-six mice by sunset all the animals have to pull together to give Mossop one last chance...

Albertine, Goose Queen

A fox is on the loose, and all the animals except Albertine the goose have hidden themselves inside. Albertine is safe on her island in the pond—at least so she thinks, until the fox starts swimming toward her...

michael morpurgo
Mudpuddle Farm

Hee-Haw Hooray!

Illustrated by
Shoo Rayner

Nothing to Worry About

There's a storm in the air, and all the animals
are worried, but old Farmer Rafferty
doesn't realize anything is wrong.
Can the animals warn him in time?

Hunky-Dory

A funny new creature arrives and the
animals soon make friends. Problem is, the
latest addition to the farm doesn't actually
belong there! It looks like it's time
to say a sad goodbye—although Albertine
the goose might just have a clever idea. . .